TWO PIANOS | FOUR HANDS

anderson & roe
DUOS & DUETS

Thr...
Two Pianos

A Medley of Waltzes
Made Famous in Disney Films
Arranged by Greg Anderson

Produced by
Alfred Music Publishing Co., Inc.
P.O. Box 10003
Van Nuys, CA 91410-0003
alfred.com

Printed in USA.

ISBN-10: 0-7390-9255-3
ISBN-13: 978-0-7390-9255-2
Cover photo
Cloudscape: © Shutterstock.com / David M. Schrader

Three Waltzes for Two Pianos
A Medley of Waltzes Made Famous in Disney Films

Arr. Greg Anderson

"Chim Chim Cher-ee" (from *Mary Poppins*)
Words and Music by Richard M. Sherman and Robert B. Sherman

(a) With the damper pedal depressed, the Piano 2 performer should lightly strum the strings inside of the piano using the pads of his or her fingers. There should be a brief silence before Piano 1 enters at the end of the bar. If the piano strings are not accessible, this alternate version can be played instead:

ⓑ Let the melody emerge gradually, as if it were "rising from the ashes."

"Someday My Prince Will Come"
Words by Larry Morey
Music by Frank Churchill

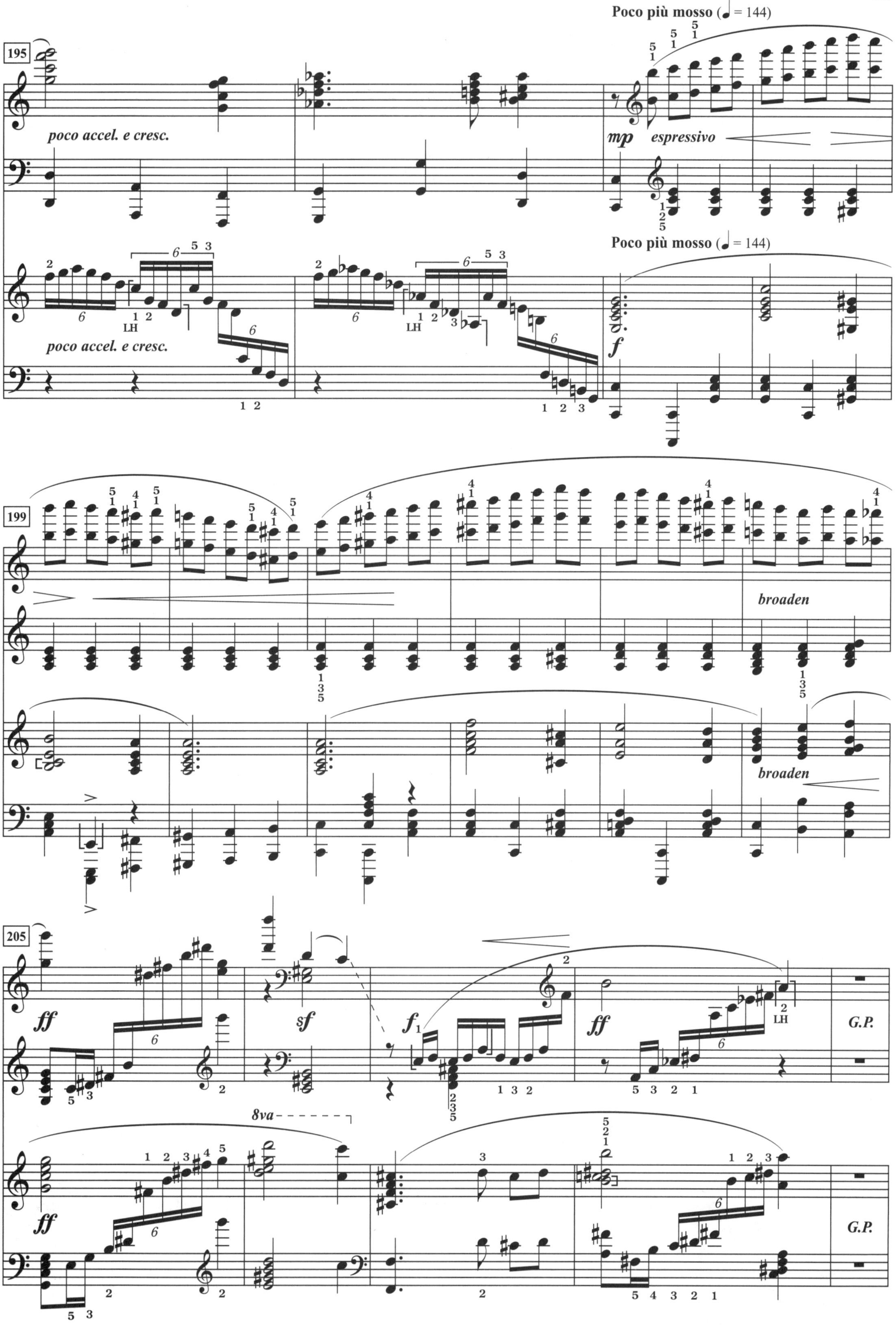
Poco più mosso (♩ = 144)
195
poco accel. e cresc.
mp
espressivo
LH
Poco più mosso (♩ = 144)
poco accel. e cresc.
f
199
broaden
broaden
205
ff
sf
f
ff
G.P.
8va
ff
G.P.

"Gaston" (from Walt Disney's *Beauty and the Beast*)
Music by Alan Menken
Lyrics by Howard Ashman

© Play the RH notes quickly, like inverted mordents.